No Great Magic

No Great Magic

by Fritz Leiber

ISBN 979-8-8809-0889-9

I

To bring the dead to life
Is no great magic.
Few are wholly dead:
Blow on a dead man's embers
And a live flame will start. —Graves

I dipped through the filmy curtain into the boys' half of the dressing room and there was Sid sitting at the star's dressing table in his threadbare yellowed undershirt, the lucky one, not making up yet but staring sternly at himself in the bulb-framed mirror and experimentally working his features a little, as actors will, and kneading the stubble on his fat chin.

I said to him quietly, "Siddy, what are we putting on tonight? Maxwell Anderson's Elizabeth the Queen or Shakespeare's Macbeth? It says Macbeth on the callboard, but Miss Nefer's getting ready for Elizabeth. She just had me go and fetch the red wig."

He tried out a few eyebrow rears—right, left, both together—then turned to me, sucking in his big gut a little, as he always does when a gal heaves into hailing distance, and said, "Your pardon, sweetling, what sayest thou?"

Sid always uses that kook antique patter backstage, until I sometimes wonder whether I'm in Central Park, New York City, nineteen hundred and three quarters, or somewhere in Southwark, Merry England, fifteen hundred and same. The truth is that although he loves every last fat part in Shakespeare and will play the skinniest one with loyal and inspired affection, he thinks Willy S. penned Falstaff with nobody else in mind but Sidney J. Lessingham. (And no accent on the ham, please.)

I closed my eyes and counted to eight, then repeated my question.

He replied, "Why, the Bard's tragical history of the bloody Scot, certes." He waved his hand toward the portrait of Shakespeare that always sits beside his mirror on top of his reserve makeup box. At first that particular picture of the Bard looked too nancy to me—a sort of peeping-tom schoolteacher—but I've grown used to it over the months and even palsy-feeling.

He didn't ask me why I hadn't asked Miss Nefer my question. Everybody in the company knows she spends the hour before curtain-time getting into character, never parting her lips except for that purpose—or to bite your head off if you try to make the most necessary conversation.

"Aye, 'tiz Macbeth tonight," Sid confirmed, returning to his frowning-practice: left eyebrow up, right down, reverse, repeat, rest. "And I must play the ill-starred Thane of Glamis."

I said, "That's fine, Siddy, but where does it leave us with Miss Nefer? She's already thinned her eyebrows and beaked out the top of her nose for Queen Liz, though that's as far as she's got. A beautiful job, the nose. Anybody else would think it was plastic surgery instead of putty. But it's going to look kind of funny on the Thaness of Glamis."

Sid hesitated a half second longer than he usually would—I thought, his timing's off tonight—and then he harrumphed and said, "Why, Iris Nefer, decked out as Good Queen Bess, will speak a prologue to the play—a prologue which I have myself but last week writ." He owled his eyes. "'Tis an experiment in the new theater."

I said, "Siddy, prologues were nothing new to Shakespeare. He had them on half his other plays. Besides, it doesn't make sense to use Queen Elizabeth. She was dead by the time he whipped up Macbeth, which is all about witchcraft and directed at King James."

He growled a little at me and demanded, "Prithee, how comes it your peewit-brain bears such a ballast of fusty book-knowledge, chit?"

I said softly, "Siddy, you don't camp in a Shakespearean dressing room for a year, tete-a-teting with some of the wisest actors ever, without learning a little. Sure I'm a mental case, a poor little A & A existing on your sweet charity, and don't think I don't appreciate it, but—"

"A-and-A, thou sayest?" he frowned. "Methinks the gladsome new forswearers of sack and ale call themselves AA."

"Agoraphobe and Amnesiac," I told him. "But look, Siddy, I was going to sayest that I do know the plays. Having Queen Elizabeth speak a prologue to Macbeth is as much an anachronism as if you put her on the gantry of the British moonship, busting a bottle of champagne over its schnozzle."

"Ha!" he cried as if he'd caught me out. "And saying there's a new Elizabeth, wouldn't that be the bravest advertisement ever for the Empire?—perchance rechristening the pilot, copilot and astrogator Drake, Hawkins and Raleigh? And the ship The Golden Hind? Tilly fally, lady!"

He went on, "My prologue an anachronism, quotha! The groundlings will never mark it. Think'st thou wisdom came to mankind with the stenchful rocket and the sundered atomy? More, the Bard himself was topfull of anachronism. He put spectacles on King Lear, had clocks tolling the hour in Caesar's Rome, buried that Roman 'stead o' burning him and gave Czechoslovakia a seacoast. Go to, doll."

"Czechoslovakia, Siddy?"

"Bohemia, then, what skills it? Leave me now, sweet poppet. Go thy ways. I have matters of import to ponder. There's more to running a repertory company than reading the footnotes to Furness."

Martin had just slouched by calling the Half Hour and looking in his solemnity, sneakers, levis and dirty T-shirt more like an underage refugee from Skid Row than Sid's newest recruit, assistant stage manager and hardest-worked juvenile—though for once he'd remembered to shave. I was about to ask Sid who was going to play Lady Mack if Miss Nefer wasn't, or, if she were going to double the roles, shouldn't I help her with the change? She's a slow dresser and the Elizabeth costumes are pretty realistically stayed. And she would have trouble getting off that nose, I was sure. But then I saw that Siddy was already slapping on the alboline to keep the grease paint from getting into his pores.

Greta, you ask too many questions, I told myself. You get everybody riled up and you rack your own poor ricketty little mind; and I hied myself off to the costumery to settle my nerves.

The costumery, which occupies the back end of the dressing room, is exactly the right place to settle the nerves and warm the fancies of any child, including an unraveled adult who's saving what's left of her sanity by pretending to be one. To begin with there are the regular costumes for Shakespeare's plays, all jeweled and spangled and brocaded, stage armor, great Roman togas with weights in the borders to make them drape right, velvets of every color to rest your cheek against and dream, and the fantastic costumes for the other plays we favor; Ibsen's Peer Gynt, Shaw's Back to Methuselah and Hilliard's adaptation of Heinlein's Children of Methuselah, the Capek brothers' Insect People, O'Neill's The Fountain, Flecker's Hassan, Camino Real, Children of the Moon, The Beggar's Opera, Mary of Scotland, Berkeley Square, The Road to Rome.

There are also the costumes for all the special and variety performances we give of the plays: Hamlet in modern dress, Julius Caesar set in a dictatorship of the 1920's, The Taming of the Shrew in caveman furs and leopard skins, where Petruchio comes in riding a dinosaur, The Tempest set on another planet with a spaceship wreck to start it off Karrumph!—which means a half dozen spacesuits, featherweight but looking ever so practical, and the weirdest sort of extraterrestrial-beast outfits for Ariel and Caliban and the other monsters.

Oh, I tell you the stuff in the costumery ranges over such a sweep of space and time that you sometimes get frightened you'll be whirled up and spun off just anywhere, so that you have to clutch at something very real to you to keep it from happening and to remind you where you really are—as I did now at the subway token on the thin gold chain around my neck (Siddy's first gift to me that I can remember) and chanted very softly to myself, like a charm or a prayer, closing my eyes and squeezing the holes in the token: "Columbus Circle, Times Square, Penn Station, Christopher Street...."

But you don't ever get really frightened in the costumery. Not exactly, though your goosehairs get wonderfully realistically tingled and your tummy chilled from time to time—because you know it's all make-believe, a lifesize doll world, a children's dress-up world. It gets you thinking of far-off times and scenes as pleasant places and not as black hungry mouths that might gobble you up and keep you forever. It's always safe, always just in the theatre, just on the stage, no matter how far it seems to plunge and roam ... and the best sort of therapy for a pot-holed mind like mine, with as many gray ruts and curves and gaps as its cerebrum, that can't remember one single thing before this last year in the dressing room and that can't ever push its shaking body out of that same motherly fatherly room, except to stand in the wings for a scene or two and watch the play until the fear gets too great and the urge to take just one peek at the audience gets too strong ... and I remember what happened the two times I did peek, and I have to come scuttling back.

The costumery's good occupational therapy for me, too, as my pricked and calloused fingertips testify. I think I must have stitched up or darned half the costumes in it this last twelvemonth, though there are so many of them that I swear the drawers have accordion pleats and the racks extend into the fourth dimension—not to mention the boxes of props and the shelves of scripts and prompt-copies and other books, including a couple of encyclopedias and the many thick volumes of Furness's Variorum Shakespeare, which as Sid had guessed I'd been boning up on. Oh, and I've sponged and pressed enough costumes, too, and even refitted them to newcomers like Martin, ripping up and resewing seams, which can be a punishing job with heavy materials.

In a less sloppily organized company I'd be called wardrobe mistress, I guess. Except that to anyone in show business that suggests a crotchety old dame with lots of authority and scissors hanging around her neck on a string. Although I got my crochets, all right, I'm not that old. Kind of childish, in fact. As for authority, everybody outranks me, even Martin.

Of course to somebody outside show business, wardrobe mistress might suggest a yummy gal who spends her time dressing up as Nell Gwyn or Anitra or Mrs. Pinchwife or Cleopatra or even Eve (we got a legal costume for it) and inspiring the boys. I've tried that once or twice. But Siddy frowns on it, and if Miss Nefer ever caught me at it I think she'd whang me.

And in a normaller company it would be the wardrobe room, too, but costumery is my infantile name for it and the actors go along with my little whims.

I don't mean to suggest our company is completely crackers. To get as close to Broadway even as Central Park you got to have something. But in spite of Sid's whip-cracking there is a comforting looseness about its efficiency—people trade around the parts they play without fuss, the bill may be changed a half hour before curtain without anybody getting hysterics, nobody gets fired for eating garlic and breathing it in the leading lady's face. In short, we're a team. Which is funny when you come to think of it, as Sid and Miss Nefer and Bruce and Maudie are British (Miss Nefer with a touch of Eurasian blood, I romance); Martin and Beau and me are American (at least I think I am) while the rest come from just everywhere.

Besides my costumery work, I fetch things and run inside errands and help the actresses dress and the actors too. The dressing room's very coeducational in a halfway respectable way. And every once in a while Martin and I police up the whole place, me skittering about with dustcloth and wastebasket, he wielding the scrub-brush and mop with such silent grim efficiency that it always makes me nervous to get through and duck back into the costumery to collect myself.

Yes, the costumery's a great place to quiet your nerves or improve your mind or even dream your life away. But this time I couldn't have been there eight minutes when Miss Nefer's Elizabeth-angry voice came skirling, "Girl! Girl! Greta, where is my ruff with silver trim?" I laid my hands on it in a flash and loped it to her, because Old Queen Liz was known to slap even her Maids of Honor around a bit now and then and Miss Nefer is a bear on getting into character—a real Paul Muni.

She was all made up now, I was happy to note, at least as far as her face went—I hate to see that spooky eight-spoked faint tattoo on her forehead (I've sometimes wondered if she got it acting in India or Egypt maybe).

Yes, she was already all made up. This time she'd been going extra heavy on the burrowing-into-character bit, I could tell right away, even if it was only for a hacked-out anachronistic prologue. She signed to me to help her dress without even looking at me, but as I got busy I looked at her eyes. They were so cold and sad and lonely (maybe because they were so far away from her eyebrows and temples and small tight mouth, and so shut away from each other by that ridge of nose) that I got the creeps. Then she began to murmur and sigh, very softly at first, then loudly enough so I got the sense of it.

"Cold, so cold," she said, still seeing things far away though her hands were working smoothly with mine. "Even a gallop hardly fires my blood. Never was such a Januarius, though there's no snow. Snow will not come, or tears. Yet my brain burns with the thought of Mary's death-warrant unsigned. There's my particular hell!—to doom, perchance, all future queens, or leave a hole for the Spaniard and the Pope to creep like old worms back into the sweet apple of England. Philip's tall black crooked ships massing like sea-going fortresses south-away—cragged castles set to march into the waves. Parma in the Lowlands! And all the while my bright young idiot gentlemen spurting out my treasure as if it were so much water, as if gold pieces were a glut of summer posies. Oh, alackanight!"

And I thought, Cry Iced!—that's sure going to be one tyrannosaur of a prologue. And how you'll ever shift back to being Lady Mack beats me. Greta, if this is what it takes to do just a bit part, you'd better give up your secret ambition of playing walk-ons some day when your nerves heal.

She was really getting to me, you see, with that characterization. It was as if I'd managed to go out and take a walk and sat down in the park outside and heard the President talking to himself about the chances of war with Russia and realized he'd sat

down on a bench with its back to mine and only a
bush between. You see, here we were, two females
undignifiedly twisted together, at the moment
getting her into that crazy crouch-deep bodice
that's like a big icecream cone, and yet here at the
same time was Queen Elizabeth the First of
England, three hundred and umpty-ump years
dead, coming back to life in a Central Park dressing
room. It shook me.

She looked so much the part, you see—even
without the red wig yet, just powdered pale makeup
going back to a quarter of an inch from her own
short dark bang combed and netted back tight. The
age too. Miss Nefer can't be a day over forty—well,
forty-two at most—but now she looked and talked
and felt to my hands dressing her, well, at least a
dozen years older. I guess when Miss Nefer gets into
character she does it with each molecule.

That age point fascinated me so much that I
risked asking her a question. Probably I was figuring
that she couldn't do me much damage because of
the positions we happened to be in at the moment.
You see, I'd started to lace her up and to do it right
I had my knee against the tail of her spine.

"How old, I mean how young might your majesty
be?" I asked her, innocently wonderingly like some
dumb serving wench.

For a wonder she didn't somehow swing around and clout me, but only settled into character a little more deeply.

"Fifty-four winters," she replied dismally. "'Tiz Januarius of Our Lord's year One Thousand and Five Hundred and Eighty and Seven. I sit cold in Greenwich, staring at the table where Mary's death warrant waits only my sign manual. If I send her to the block, I open the doors to future, less official regicides. But if I doom her not, Philip's armada will come inching up the Channel in a season, puffing smoke and shot, and my English Catholics, thinking only of Mary Regina, will rise and i' the end the Spaniard will have all. All history would alter. That must not be, even if I'm damned for it! And yet ... and yet...."

A bright blue fly came buzzing along (the dressing room has some insect life) and slowly circled her head rather close, but she didn't even flicker her eyelids.

"I sit cold in Greenwich, going mad. Each afternoon I ride, praying for some mischance, some prodigy, to wash from my mind away the bloody question for some little space. It skills not what: a fire, a tree a-failing, Davison or e'en Eyes Leicester tumbled with his horse, an assassin's ball clipping the cold twigs by my ear, a maid crying rape, a wild boar charging with dipping tusks, news of the Spaniard at Thames' mouth or, more happily, a band of strolling actors setting forth some new comedy to charm the fancy or some great unheard-of tragedy to tear the heart—though that were somewhat much to hope for at this season and place, even if Southwark be close by."

The lacing was done. I stood back from her, and really she looked so much like Elizabeth painted by Gheeraerts or on the Great Seal of Ireland or something—though the ash-colored plush dress trimmed in silver and the little silver-edge ruff and the black-silver tinsel-cloth cloak lined with white plush hanging behind her looked most like a winter riding costume—and her face was such a pale frozen mask of Elizabeth's inward tortures, that I told myself, Oh, I got to talk to Siddy again, he's made some big mistake, the lardy old lackwit. Miss Nefer just can't be figuring on playing in Macbeth tonight.

As a matter of fact I was nerving myself to ask her all about it direct, though it was going to take some real nerve and maybe be risking broken bones or at least a flayed cheek to break the ice of that characterization, when who should come by calling the Fifteen Minutes but Martin. He looked so downright goofy that it took my mind off Nefer-in-character for all of eight seconds.

His levied bottom half still looked like The Lower Depths. Martin is Village Stanislavsky rather than Ye Olde English Stage Traditions. But above that

... well, all it really amounted to was that he was stripped to the waist and had shaved off the small high tuft of chest hair and was wearing a black wig that hung down in front of his shoulders in two big braids heavy with silver hoops and pins. But just the same those simple things, along with his tarpaper-solarium tan and habitual poker expression, made him look so like an American Indian that I thought, Hey Zeus!—he's all set to play Hiawatha, or if he'd just cover up that straight-line chest, a frowny Pocahontas. And I quick ran through what plays with Indian parts we do and could only come up with The Fountain.

I mutely goggled my question at him, wiggling my hands like guppy fins, but he brushed me off with a solemn mysterious smile and backed through the curtain. I thought, nobody can explain this but Siddy, and I followed Martin.

II

History does not move in one current,
like the wind across bare seas,
but in a thousand streams and eddies,
like the wind over a broken landscape.—Cary

The boys' half of the dressing room (two-thirds really) was bustling. There was the smell of spirit gum and Max Factor and just plain men. Several guys were getting dressed or un—, and Bruce was cussing Bloody-something because he'd just burnt his fingers unwinding from the neck of a hot electric bulb some crepe hair he'd wound there to dry after wetting and stretching it to turn it from crinkly to straight for his Banquo beard. Bruce is always getting to the theater late and trying shortcuts.

But I had eyes only for Sid. So help me, as soon as I saw him they bugged again. Greta, I told myself, you're going to have to send Martin out to the drugstore for some anti-bug powder. "For the roaches, boy?" "No, for the eyes."

Sid was made up and had his long mustaches and elf-locked Macbeth wig on—and his corset too. I could tell by the way his waist was sucked in before he saw me. But instead of dark kilts and that bronze-studded sweat-stained leather battle harness that lets him show off his beefy shoulders and the top half of his heavily furred chest—and which really does look great on Macbeth in the first act when he comes in straight from battle—but instead of that he was wearing, so help me, red tights cross-gartered with strips of gold-blue tinsel-cloth, a green doublet gold-trimmed and to top it a ruff, and he was trying to fit onto his front a bright silvered cuirass that would have looked just dandy maybe on one of the Pope's Swiss Guards.

I thought, Siddy, Willy S. ought to reach out of his portrait there and bop you one on the koko for contemplating such a crazy-quilt desecration of just about his greatest and certainly his most atmospheric play.

Just then he noticed me and hissed accusingly, "There thou art, slothy minx! Spring to and help stuff me into this monstrous chest-kettle."

"Siddy, what is all this?" I demanded as my hands automatically obeyed. "Are you going to play Macbeth for laughs, except maybe leaving the Porter a serious character? You think you're Red Skelton?"

Elizabeth

"What monstrous brabble is this, you mad bitch?" he retorted, grunting as I bear-hugged his waist, shouldering the cuirass to squeeze it home.

"The clown costumes on all you men," I told him, for now I'd noticed that the others were in rainbow hues, Bruce a real eye-buster in yellow tights and violet doublet as he furiously bushed out and clipped crosswise sections of beard and slapped them on his chin gleaming brown with spirit gum. "I haven't seen any eight-inch polka-dots yet but I'm sure I will."

Suddenly a big grin split Siddy's face and he laughed out loud at me, though the laugh changed to a gasp as I strapped in the cuirass three notches too tight. When we'd got that adjusted he said, "I' faith thou slayest me, pretty witling. Did I not tell you this production is an experiment, a novelty?

We shall but show Macbeth as it might have been costumed at the court of King James. In the clothes of the day, but gaudier, as was then the stage fashion. Hold, dove, I've somewhat for thee." He fumbled his grouch bag from under his doublet and dipped finger and thumb in it, and put in my palm a silver model of the Empire State Building, charm bracelet size, and one of the new Kennedy dimes.

As I squeezed those two and gloated my eyes on them, feeling securer and happier and friendlier for them though I didn't at the moment want to, I thought, Well, Siddy's right about that, at least I've read they used to costume the plays that way, though I don't see how Shakespeare stood it. But it was dirty of them all not to tell me beforehand.

But that's the way it is. Sometimes I'm the butt as well as the pet of the dressing room, and considering all the breaks I get I shouldn't mind. I smiled at Sid and went on tiptoes and necked out my head and kissed him on a powdery cheek just above an aromatic mustache. Then I wiped the smile off my face and said, "Okay, Siddy, play Macbeth as Little Lord Fauntleroy or Baby Snooks if you want to. I'll never squeak again. But the Elizabeth prologue's still an anachronism. And—this is the thing I came to tell you, Siddy—Miss Nefer's not getting ready for any measly prologue. She's set to play Queen Elizabeth all night and tomorrow morning too. Whatever you think, she doesn't know we're doing Macbeth. But who'll do Lady Mack if she doesn't? And Martin's not dressing for Malcolm, but for the Son of the Last of the Mohicans, I'd say. What's more—"

You know, something I said must have annoyed Sid, for he changed his mood again in a flash. "Shut your jaw, you crook brained cat, and begone!" he snarled at me. "Here's curtain time close upon us, and you come like a wittol scattering your mad questions like the crazed Ophelia her flowers. Begone, I say!"

"Yessir," I whipped out softly. I skittered off toward the door to the stage, because that was the easiest direction. I figured I could do with a breath of less grease-painty air. Then, "Oh, Greta," I heard Martin call nicely.

He'd changed his levis for black tights, and was stepping into and pulling up around him a very familiar dress, dark green and embroidered with silver and stage-rubies. He'd safety-pinned a folded towel around his chest—to make a bosom of sorts, I realized.

He armed into the sleeves and turned his back to me. "Hook me up, would you?" he entreated.

Then it hit me. They had no actresses in Shakespeare's day, they used boys. And the dark green dress was so familiar to me because—

"Martin," I said, halfway up the hooks and working fast—Miss Nefer's costume fitted him fine. "You're going to play—?"

"Lady Macbeth, yes," he finished for me. "Wish me courage, will you Greta? Nobody else seems to think I need it."

I punched him half-heartedly in the rear. Then, as I fastened the last hooks, my eyes topped his shoulder and I looked at our faces side by side in the mirror of his dressing table. His, in spite of the female edging and him being at least eight years younger than me, I think, looked wise, poised, infinitely resourceful with power in reserve, very very real, while mine looked like that of a bewildered and characterless child ghost about to scatter into air—and the edges of my charcoal sweater and skirt, contrasting with his strong colors, didn't dispel that last illusion.

"Oh, by the way, Greta," he said, "I picked up a copy of The Village Times for you. There's a thumbnail review of our Measure for Measure, though it mentions no names, darn it. It's around here somewhere...."

But I was already hurrying on. Oh, it was logical enough to have Martin playing Mrs. Macbeth in a production styled to Shakespeare's own times (though pedantically over-authentic, I'd have thought) and it really did answer all my questions, even why Miss Nefer could sink herself wholly in

Elizabeth tonight if she wanted to. But it meant that I must be missing so much of what was going on right around me, in spite of spending 24 hours a day in the dressing room, or at most in the small adjoining john or in the wings of the stage just outside the dressing room door, that it scared me. Siddy telling everybody, "Macbeth tonight in Elizabethan costume, boys and girls," sure, that I could have missed—though you'd have thought he'd have asked my help on the costumes.

But Martin getting up in Mrs. Mack. Why, someone must have held the part on him twenty-eight times, cueing him, while he got the lines. And there must have been at least a couple of run-through rehearsals to make sure he had all the business and stage movements down pat, and Sid and Martin would have been doing their big scenes every backstage minute they could spare with Sid yelling, "Witling! Think'st that's a wifely buss?" and Martin would have been droning his lines last time he scrubbed and mopped....

Greta, they're hiding things from you, I told myself.

Maybe there was a 25th hour nobody had told me about yet when they did all the things they didn't tell me about.

Maybe they were things they didn't dare tell me because of my top-storey weakness.

I felt a cold draft and shivered and I realized I was at the door to the stage.

I should explain that our stage is rather an unusual one, in that it can face two ways, with the drops and set pieces and lighting all capable of being switched around completely. To your left, as you look out the dressing-room door, is an open-air theater, or rather an open-air place for the audience—a large upward-sloping glade walled by thick tall trees and with benches for over two thousand people. On that side the stage kind of merges into the grass and can be made to look part of it by a green groundcloth.

To your right is a big roofed auditorium with the same number of seats.

The whole thing grew out of the free summer Shakespeare performances in Central Park that they started back in the 1950's.

The Janus-stage idea is that in nice weather you can have the audience outdoors, but if it rains or there's a cold snap, or if you want to play all winter without a single break, as we've been doing, then you can put your audience in the auditorium. In that case, a big accordion-pleated wall shuts off the out of doors and keeps the wind from blowing your backdrop, which is on that side, of course, when the auditorium's in use.

Tonight the stage was set up to face the outdoors, although that draft felt mighty chilly.

I hesitated, as I always do at the door to the stage—though it wasn't the actual stage lying just ahead of me, but only backstage, the wings. You see, I always have to fight the feeling that if I go out the dressing room door, go out just eight steps, the world will change while I'm out there and I'll never be able to get back. It won't be New York City any more, but Chicago or Mars or Algiers or Atlanta, Georgia, or Atlantis or Hell and I'll never be able to get back to that lovely warm womb with all the jolly boys and girls and all the costumes smelling like autumn leaves.

Or, especially when there's a cold breeze blowing, I'm afraid that I'll change, that I'll grow wrinkled and old in eight footsteps, or shrink down to the witless blob of a baby, or forget altogether who I am—

—or, it occurred to me for the first time now, remember who I am. Which might be even worse.

Maybe that's what I'm afraid of.

I took a step back. I noticed something new just beside the door: a high-legged, short-keyboard piano. Then I saw that the legs were those of a table. The piano was just a box with yellowed keys. Spinet? Harpsichord?

"Five minutes, everybody," Martin quietly called out behind me.

I took hold of myself. Greta, I told myself—also for the first time, you know that some day you're really going to have to face this thing, and not just for a quick dip out and back either. Better get in some practice.

I stepped through the door.

Beau and Doc were already out there, made up and in costume for Ross and King Duncan. They were discreetly peering past the wings at the gathering audience. Or at the place where the audience ought to be gathering, at any rate—sometimes the movies and girlie shows and brainheavy beatnik bruhahas outdraw us altogether. Their costumes were the same kooky colorful ones as the others'. Doc had a mock-ermine robe and a huge gilt papier-mache crown. Beau was carrying a ragged black robe and hood over his left arm—he doubles the First Witch.

As I came up behind them, making no noise in my black sneakers, I heard Beau say, "I see some rude fellows from the City approaching. I was hoping we wouldn't get any of those. How should they scent us out?"

Brother, I thought, where do you expect them to come from if not the City? Central Park is bounded on three sides by Manhattan Island and on the fourth by the Eighth Avenue Subway. And Brooklyn and Bronx boys have got pretty sharp scenters. And what's it get you insulting the woiking and non-woiking people of the woild's greatest metropolis? Be grateful for any audience you get, boy.

But I suppose Beau Lassiter considers anybody from north of Vicksburg a "rude fellow" and is always waiting for the day when the entire audience will arrive in carriage and democrat wagons.

Doc replied, holding down his white beard and heavy on the mongrel Russo-German accent he miraculously manages to suppress on stage except when "Vot does it matter? Ve don't convinze zem, ve don't convinze nobody. Nichevo."

Maybe, I thought, Doc shares my doubts about making Macbeth plausible in rainbow pants.

Still unobserved by them, I looked between their shoulders and got the first of my shocks.

It wasn't night at all, but afternoon. A dark cold lowering afternoon, admittedly. But afternoon all the same.

Sure, between shows I sometimes forget whether it's day or night, living inside like I do. But getting matinees and evening performances mixed is something else again.

It also seemed to me, although Beau was leaning in now and I couldn't see so well, that the glade was smaller than it should be, the trees closer to us and more irregular, and I couldn't see the benches. That was Shock Two.

Beau said anxiously, glancing at his wrist, "I wonder what's holding up the Queen?"

Although I was busy keeping up nerve-pressure against the shocks, I managed to think. So he knows about Siddy's stupid Queen Elizabeth prologue too. But of course he would. It's only me they keep in the dark. If he's so smart he ought to remember that Miss Nefer is always the last person on stage, even when she opens the play.

And then I thought I heard, through the trees, the distant drumming of horses' hoofs and the sound of a horn.

Now they do have horseback riding in Central Park and you can hear auto horns there, but the hoofbeats don't drum that wild way. And there aren't so many riding together. And no auto horn I ever heard gave out with that sweet yet imperious ta-ta-ta-TA.

I must have squeaked or something, because Beau and Doc turned around quickly, blocking my view, their expressions half angry, half anxious.

I turned too and ran for the dressing room, for I could feel one of my mind-wavery fits coming on. At the last second it had seemed to me that the scenery was getting skimpier, hardly more than thin trees and bushes itself, and underfoot feeling more like ground than a ground cloth, and overhead not theater roof but gray sky. Shock Three and you're out, Greta, my umpire was calling.

I made it through the dressing room door and nothing there was wavering or dissolving, praised be

Pan. Just Martin standing with his back to me, alert, alive, poised like a cat inside that green dress, the prompt book in his right hand with a finger in it, and from his left hand long black tatters swinging—telling me he'd still be doubling Second Witch. And he was hissing, "Places, please, everybody. On stage!"

With a sweep of silver and ash-colored plush, Miss Nefer came past him, for once leading the last-minute hurry to the stage. She had on the dark red wig now. For me that crowned her characterization. It made me remember her saying, "My brain burns." I ducked aside as if she were majesty incarnate.

And then she didn't break her own precedent. She stopped at the new thing beside the door and poised her long white skinny fingers over the yellowed keys, and suddenly I remembered what it was called: a virginals.

She stared down at it fiercely, evilly, like a witch planning an enchantment. Her face got the secret fiendish look that, I told myself, the real Elizabeth would have had ordering the deaths of Ballard and Babington, or plotting with Drake (for all they say she didn't) one of his raids, that long long forefinger tracing crooked courses through a crabbedly drawn map of the Indies and she smiling at the dots of cities that would burn.

Then all her eight fingers came flickering down and the strings inside the virginals began to twang and hum with a high-pitched rendering of Grieg's "In the Hall of the Mountain King."

Then as Sid and Bruce and Martin rushed past me, along with a black swooping that was Maud already robed and hooded for Third Witch, I beat it for my sleeping closet like Peer Gynt himself dashing across the mountainside away from the cave of the Troll King, who only wanted to make tiny slits in his eyeballs so that forever afterwards he'd see reality just a little differently. And as I ran, the master-anachronism of that menacing mad march music was shrilling in my ears.

III

Sound a dumbe shew. Enter the three fatall sisters, with a rocke, a threed, and a pair of sheeres.—Old Play

My sleeping closet is just a cot at the back end of the girls' third of the dressing room, with a three-panel screen to make it private.

When I sleep I hang my outside clothes on the screen, which is pasted and thumbtacked all over with the New York City stuff that gives me security: theater programs and restaurant menus, clippings from the Times and the Mirror, a torn-out picture of the United Nations building with a hundred tiny gay paper flags pasted around it, and hanging in an old hairnet a home-run baseball autographed by Willy Mays. Things like that.

Right now I was jumping my eyes over that stuff, asking it to keep me located and make me safe, as I lay on my cot in my clothes with my knees drawn up and my fingers over my ears so the louder lines from the play wouldn't be able to come nosing back around the trunks and tables and bright-lit mirrors and find me. Generally I like to listen to them, even if they're sort of sepulchral and drained of overtones by their crooked trip. But they're always tense-making. And tonight (I mean this afternoon)—no!

It's funny I should find security in mementos of a city I daren't go out into—no, not even for a stroll through Central Park, though I know it from the Pond to Harlem Meer—the Met Museum, the Menagerie, the Ramble, the Great Lawn, Cleopatra's Needle and all the rest. But that's the way it is. Maybe I'm like Jonah in the whale, reluctant to go outside because the whale's a terrible monster that's awful scary to look in the face and might really damage you gulping you a second time, yet reassured to know you're living in the stomach of that particular monster and not a seventeen tentacled one from the fifth planet of Aldebaran.

It's really true, you see, about me actually living in the dressing room. The boys bring me meals: coffee in cardboard cylinders and doughnuts in little brown grease-spotted paper sacks and malts and hamburgers and apples and little pizzas, and Maud brings me raw vegetables—carrots and parsnips and little onions and such, and watches to make sure I exercise my molars grinding them and get my vitamins. I take spit-baths in the little john. Architects don't seem to think actors ever take baths, even when they've browned themselves all over playing Pindarus the Parthian in Julius Caesar. And all my shut-eye is caught on this little cot in the twilight of my NYC screen.

You'd think I'd be terrified being alone in the dressing room during the wee and morning hours, let alone trying to sleep then, but that isn't the way it works out. For one thing, there's apt to be someone sleeping in too. Maudie especially. And it's my favorite time too for costume-mending and reading the Variorum and other books, and for just plain way-out dreaming. You see, the dressing room is the one place I really do feel safe. Whatever is out there in New York that terrorizes me, I'm pretty confident that it can never get in here.

Besides that, there's a great big bolt on the inside of the dressing room door that I throw whenever I'm all alone after the show. Next day they buzz for me to open it.

It worried me a bit at first and I had asked Sid, "But what if I'm so deep asleep I don't hear and you have to get in fast?" and he had replied, "Sweetling, a word in your ear: our own Beauregard Lassiter is the prettiest picklock unjailed since Jimmy Valentine and Jimmy Dale. I'll not ask where he learned his trade, but 'tis sober truth, upon my honor."

And Beau had confirmed this with a courtly bow, murmuring, "At your service, Miss Greta."

"How do you jigger a big iron bolt through a three-inch door that fits like Maudie's tights?" I wanted to know.

"He carries lodestones of great power and divers subtle tools," Sid had explained for him.

I don't know how they work it so that some Traverse-Three cop or park official doesn't find out about me and raise a stink. Maybe Sid just throws a little more of the temperament he uses to keep most outsiders out of the dressing-room. We sure don't get any janitors or scrubwomen, as Martin and I know only too well. More likely he squares someone. I do get the impression all the company's gone a little way out on a limb letting me stay here—that the directors of our theater wouldn't like it if they found out about me.

In fact, the actors are all so good about helping me and putting up with my antics (though they have their own, Danu digs!) that I sometimes think

I must be related to one of them—a distant cousin or sister-in-law (or wife, my God!), because I've checked our faces side by side in the mirrors often enough and I can't find any striking family resemblances. Or maybe I was even an actress in the company. The least important one. Playing the tiniest roles like Lucius in Caesar and Bianca in Othello and one of the little princes in Dick the Three Eyes and Fleance and the Gentlewoman in Macbeth, though me doing even that much acting strikes me to laugh.

But whatever I am in that direction—if I'm anything—not one of the actors has told me a word about it or dropped the least hint. Not even when I beg them to tell me or try to trick them into it, presumably because it might revive the shock that gave me agoraphobia and amnesia in the first place, and maybe this time knock out my entire mind or at least smash the new mouse-in-a-hole consciousness I've made for myself.

I guess they must have got by themselves a year ago and talked me over and decided my best chance for cure or for just bumping along half happily was staying in the dressing room rather than being sent home (funny, could I have another?) or to a mental hospital. And then they must have been cocky enough about their amateur psychiatry and interested enough in me (the White

Horse knows why) to go ahead with a program almost any psychiatrist would be bound to yike at.

I got so worried about the set up once and about the risks they might be running that, gritting down my dread of the idea, I said to Sid, "Siddy, shouldn't I see a doctor?"

He looked at me solemnly for a couple of seconds and then said, "Sure, why not? Go talk to Doc right now," tipping a thumb toward Doc Pyeskov, who was just sneaking back into the bottom of his makeup box what looked like a half pint from the flask I got. I did, incidentally. Doc explained to me Kraepelin's classification of the psychoses, muttering, as he absentmindedly fondled my wrist, that in a year or two he'd be a good illustration of Korsakov's Syndrome.

They've all been pretty darn good to me in their kooky ways, the actors have. Not one of them has tried to take advantage of my situation to extort anything out of me, beyond asking me to sew on a button or polish some boots or at worst clean the wash bowl. Not one of the boys has made a pass I didn't at least seem to invite. And when my crush on Sid was at its worst he shouldered me off by getting polite—something he only is to strangers. On the rebound I hit Beau, who treated me like a real Southern gentleman.

All this for a stupid little waif, whom anyone but a gang of sentimental actors would have sent to

Bellevue without a second thought or feeling. For, to get disgustingly realistic, my most plausible theory of me is that I'm a stage-struck girl from Iowa who saw her twenties slipping away and her sanity too, and made the dash to Greenwich Village, and went so ape on Shakespeare after seeing her first performance in Central Park that she kept going back there night after night (Christopher Street, Penn Station, Times Square, Columbus Circle—see?) and hung around the stage door, so mousy but open-mouthed that the actors made a pet of her.

And then something very nasty happened to her, either down at the Village or in a dark corner of the Park. Something so nasty that it blew the top of her head right off. And she ran to the only people and place where she felt she could ever again feel safe. And she showed them the top of her head with its singed hair and its jagged ring of skull and they took pity.

My least plausible theory of me, but the one I like the most, is that I was born in the dressing room, cradled in the top of a flat theatrical trunk with my ears full of Shakespeare's lines before I ever said "Mama," let alone lamped a TV; hush-walked when I cried by whoever was off stage, old props my first toys, trying to eat crepe hair my first indiscretion, sticks of grease-paint my first crayons. You know, I really wouldn't be bothered by crazy fears about New York changing and the dressing room shifting around in space and time, if I could be sure I'd always be able to stay in it and that the same sweet guys and gals would always be with me and that the shows would always go on.

This show was sure going on, it suddenly hit me, for I'd let my fingers slip off my ears as I sentimentalized and wish-dreamed and I heard, muted by the length and stuff of the dressing room, the slow beat of a drum and then a drum note in Maudie's voice taking up that beat as she warned the other two witches, "A drum, a drum! Macbeth doth come."

Why, I'd not only missed Sid's history-making-and-breaking Queen Elizabeth prologue (kicking myself that I had, now it was over), I'd also missed the short witch scene with its famous "Fair is foul and foul is fair," the Bloody Sergeant scene where Duncan hears about Macbeth's victory, and we were well into the second witch scene, the one on the blasted heath where Macbeth gets it predicted to him he'll be king after Duncan and is tempted to speculate about hurrying up the process.

I sat up. I did hesitate a minute then, my fingers going back toward my ears, because Macbeth is specially tense-making and when I've had one of my mind-wavery fits I feel weak for a while and things are blurry and uncertain. Maybe I'd better take a couple of the barbiturate sleeping pills Maudie manages to get for me and—but No, Greta, I told myself, you want to watch this show, you want to see how they do in those crazy costumes. You especially want to see how Martin makes out. He'd never forgive you if you didn't.

So I walked to the other end of the empty dressing room, moving quite slowly and touching the edges here and there, the words of the play getting louder all the time. By the time I got to the door Bruce-Banquo was saying to the witches, "If you can look into the seeds of time, And say which grain will grow and which will not,"—those lines that stir anyone's imagination with their veiled vision of the universe.

The overall lighting was a little dim (afternoon fading already?—a late matinee?) and the stage lights flickery and the scenery still a little spectral-flimsy. Oh, my mind-wavery fits can be lulus! But I concentrated on the actors, watching them through the entrance-gaps in the wings. They were solid enough.

Giving a solid performance, too, as I decided after watching that scene through and the one after it where Duncan congratulates Macbeth, with never a pause between the two scenes in true Elizabethan style. Nobody was laughing at the colorful costumes. After a while I began to accept them myself.

Oh, it was a different Macbeth than our company usually does. Louder and faster, with shorter pauses between speeches, the blank verse at times approaching a chant. But it had a lot of real guts and everybody was just throwing themselves into it, Sid especially.

The first Lady Macbeth scene came. Without exactly realizing it I moved forward to where I'd been when I got my three shocks. Martin is so intent on his career and making good that he has me the same way about it.

The Thaness started off, as she always does, toward the opposite side of the stage and facing a little away from me. Then she moved a step and looked down at the stage-parchment letter in her hands and began to read it, though there was nothing on it but scribble, and my heart sank because the voice I heard was Miss Nefer's. I thought (and almost said out loud) Oh, dammit, he funked out, or Sid decided at the last minute he couldn't trust him with the part. Whoever got Miss Nefer out of the ice cream cone in time?

Then she swung around and I saw that no, my God, it was Martin, no mistaking. He'd been using her voice. When a person first does a part, especially getting up in it without much rehearsing, he's bound to copy the actor he's been hearing doing it. And as I listened on, I realized it was fundamentally Martin's own voice pitched a trifle

high, only some of the intonations and rhythms
were Miss Nefer's. He was showing a lot of feeling
and intensity too and real Martin-type poise. You're
off to a great start, kid, I cheered inwardly. Keep it
up!

Just then I looked toward the audience. Once
again I almost squeaked out loud. For out there,
close to the stage, in the very middle of the reserve
section, was a carpet spread out. And sitting in the
middle of it on some sort of little chair, with what
looked like two charcoal braziers smoking to either
side of her, was Miss Nefer with a string of extras in
Elizabethan hats with cloaks pulled around them.

For a second it really threw me because it
reminded me of the things I'd seen or thought I'd
seen the couple of times I'd sneaked a peek through
the curtain-hole at the audience in the indoor
auditorium.

It hardly threw me for more than a second,
though, because I remembered that the characters
who speak Shakespeare's prologues often stay on
stage and sometimes kind of join the audience and
even comment on the play from time to
time—Christopher Sly and attendant lords in The
Shrew, for one. Sid had just copied and in his usual
style laid it on thick.

Well, bully for you, Siddy, I thought, I'm sure the
witless New York groundlings will be thrilled to
their cold little toes knowing they're sitting in the

same audience as Good Queen Liz and attendant courtiers. And as for you, Miss Nefer, I added a shade invidiously, you just keep on sitting cold in Central Park, warmed by dry-ice smoke from braziers, and keep your mouth shut and everything'll be fine. I'm sincerely glad you'll be able to be Queen Elizabeth all night long. Just so long as you don't try to steal the scene from Martin and the rest of the cast, and the real play.

I suppose that camp chair will get a little uncomfortable by the time the Fifth Act comes tramping along to that drumbeat, but I'm sure you're so much in character you'll never feel it.

One thing though: just don't scare me again pretending to work witchcraft—with a virginals or any other way.

Okay?

Swell.

Me, now, I'm going to watch the play.

IV

... to dream of new dimensions,
Cheating checkmate
by painting the king's robe
So that he slides like a queen;—Graves

I swung back to the play just at the moment Lady Mack soliloquizes, "Come to my woman's breasts. And take my milk for gall, you murdering

ministers." Although I knew it was just folded towel
Martin was touching with his fingertips as he lifted
them to the top half of his green bodice, I got
carried away, he made it so real. I decided boys can
play girls better than people think. Maybe they
should do it a little more often, and girls play boys
too.

Then Sid-Macbeth came back to his wife from
the wars, looking triumphant but scared because
the murder-idea's started to smoulder in him, and
she got busy fanning the blaze like any other good
little hausfrau intent on her husband rising in the
company and knowing that she's the power behind
him and that when there are promotions someone's
always got to get the axe. Sid and Martin made this
charming little domestic scene so natural yet gutsy
too that I wanted to shout hooray. Even Sid
clutching Martin to that ridiculous pot-chested
cuirass didn't have one note of horseplay in it.
Their bodies spoke. It was the McCoy.

After that, the play began to get real good, the
fast tempo and exaggerated facial expressions
actually helping it. By the time the Dagger Scene
came along I was digging my fingernails into my
sweaty palms. Which was a good thing—my eating
up the play, I mean—because it kept me from
looking at the audience again, even taking a fast
peek. As you've gathered, audiences bug me. All
those people out there in the shadows, watching

the actors in the light, all those silent voyeurs as Bruce calls them. Why, they might be anything. And sometimes (to my mind-wavery sorrow) I think they are. Maybe crouching in the dark out there, hiding among the others, is the one who did the nasty thing to me that tore off the top of my head.

Anyhow, if I so much as glance at the audience, I begin to get ideas about it—and sometimes even if I don't, as just at this moment I thought I heard horses restlessly pawing hard ground and one whinny, though that was shut off fast. Krishna kressed us! I thought, Skiddy can't have hired horses for Nefer-Elizabeth much as he's a circus man at heart. We don't have that kind of money. Besides—

But just then Sid-Macbeth gasped as if he were sucking in a bucket of air. He'd shed the cuirass, fortunately. He said, "Is this a dagger which I see before me, the handle toward my hand?" and the play hooked me again, and I had no time to think about or listen for anything else. Most of the offstage actors were on the other side of the stage, as that's where they make their exits and entrances at this point in the Second Act. I stood alone in the wings, watching the play like a bug, frightened only of the horrors Shakespeare had in mind when he wrote it.

Yes, the play was going great. The Dagger Scene was terrific where Duncan gets murdered offstage, and so was the part afterwards where hysteria mounts as the crime's discovered.

But just at this point I began to catch notes I didn't like. Twice someone was late on entrance and came on as if shot from a cannon. And three times at least Sid had to throw someone a line when they blew up—in the clutches Sid's better than any prompt book. It began to look as if the play were getting out of control, maybe because the new tempo was so hot.

But they got through the Murder Scene okay. As they came trooping off, yelling "Well contented," most of them on my side for a change, I went for Sid with a towel. He always sweats like a pig in the Murder Scene. I mopped his neck and shoved the towel up under his doublet to catch the dripping armpits.

Meanwhile he was fumbling around on a narrow table where they lay props and costumes for quick changes. Suddenly he dug his fingers into my shoulder, enough to catch my attention at this point, meaning I'd show bruises tomorrow, and yelled at me under his breath, "And you love me, our crows and robes. Presto!"

I was off like a flash to the costumery. There were Mr. and Mrs. Mack's king-and-queen robes and stuff hanging and sitting just where I knew they'd have to be.

I snatched them up, thinking, Boy, they made a mistake when they didn't tell about this special performance, and I started back like Flash Two.

As I shot out the dressing room door the theater was very quiet. There's a short low-pitched scene on stage then, to give the audience a breather. I heard Miss Nefer say loudly (it had to be loud to get to me from even the front of the audience): "'Tis a good bloody play, Eyes," and some voice I didn't recognize reply a bit grudgingly, "There's meat in it and some poetry too, though rough-wrought." She went on, still as loudly as if she owned the theater, "'Twill make Master Kyd bite his nails with jealousy—ha, ha!"

Ha-ha yourself, you scene-stealing witch, I thought, as I helped Sid and then Martin on with their royal outer duds. But at the same time I knew Sid must have written those lines himself to go along with his prologue. They had the unmistakable rough-wrought Lessingham touch. Did he really expect the audience to make anything of that reference to Shakespeare's predecessor Thomas Kyd of The Spanish Tragedy and the lost Hamlet? And if they knew enough to spot that, wouldn't they be bound to realize the whole Elizabeth-Macbeth tie-up was anachronistic? But when Sid gets an inspiration he can be very bull-headed.

Just then, while Bruce-Banquo was speaking his broody low soliloquy on stage, Miss Nefer cut in again loudly with, "Aye, Eyes, a good bloody play. Yet somehow, methinks—I know not how—I've heard it before." Whereupon Sid grabbed Martin by the wrist and hissed, "Did'st hear? Oh, I like not that," and I thought, Oh-ho, so now she's beginning to ad-lib.

Well, right away they all went on stage with a flourish, Sid and Martin crowned and hand in hand. The play got going strong again. But there were still those edge-of-control undercurrents and I began to be more uneasy than caught up, and I had to stare consciously at the actors to keep off a wavery-fit.

Other things began to bother me too, such as all the doubling.

Macbeth's a great play for doubling. For instance, anyone except Macbeth or Banquo can double one of the Three Witches—or one of the Three Murderers for that matter. Normally we double at least one or two of the Witches and Murderers, but this performance there'd been more multiple-parting than I'd ever seen. Doc had whipped off his Duncan beard and thrown on a brown smock and hood to play the Porter with his normal bottle-roughened accents. Well, a drunk impersonating a drunk, pretty appropriate. But Bruce was doing the next-door-to-impossible double of Banquo and Macduff, using a ringing tenor voice for the latter and wearing in the murder scene a helmet with dropped visor to hide his Banquo beard. He'd be able to tear it off, of course, after the Murderers got Banquo and he'd made his brief appearance as a bloodied-up ghost in the Banquet Scene. I asked myself, My God, has Siddy got all the other actors out in front playing courtiers to Elizabeth-Nefer? Wasting them that way? The whoreson rogue's gone nuts!

But really it was plain frightening, all that frantic doubling and tripling with its suggestion that the play (and the company too, Freya forfend) was becoming a ricketty patchwork illusion with everybody racing around faster and faster to hide the holes. And the scenery-wavery stuff and the warped Park-sounds were scary too. I was actually shivering by the time Sid got to: "Light thickens; and the crow Makes wing to the rooky wood: Good things of day begin to droop and drowse; Whiles night's black agents to their preys do rouse." Those graveyard lines didn't help my nerves any, of course. Nor did thinking I heard Nefer-Elizabeth say from the audience, rather softly for her this time, "Eyes, I have heard that speech, I know not where. Think you 'tiz stolen?"

Greta, I told myself, you need a miltown before the crow makes wing through your kooky head.

I turned to go and fetch me one from my closet. And stopped dead.

Just behind me, pacing back and forth like an ash-colored tiger in the gloomy wings, looking daggers at the audience every time she turned at that end of her invisible cage, but ignoring me completely, was Miss Nefer in the Elizabeth wig and rig.

Well, I suppose I should have said to myself, Greta, you imagined that last loud whisper from the audience. Miss Nefer's simply unkinked herself, waved a hand to the real audience and come back stage. Maybe Sid just had her out there for the first half of the play. Or maybe she just couldn't stand watching Martin give such a bang-up performance in her part of Lady Mack.

Yes, maybe I should have told myself something like that, but somehow all I could think then—and I thought it with a steady mounting shiver—was, We got two Elizabeths. This one is our witch Nefer. I know. I dressed her. And I know that devil-look from the virginals. But if this is our Elizabeth, the company Elizabeth, the stage Elizabeth ... who's the other?

And because I didn't dare to let myself think of the answer to that question, I dodged around the invisible cage that the ash-colored skirt seemed to ripple against as the Tiger Queen turned and I ran into the dressing room, my only thought to get behind my New York City Screen.

V

Even little things are turning out to be great things and becoming intensely interesting.

Have you ever thought about the properties of numbers?—The Maiden

Lying on my cot, my eyes crosswise to the printing, I looked from a pink Algonquin menu to a pale green New Amsterdam program, with a tiny doll of Father Knickerbocker dangling between them on a yellow thread. Really they weren't covering up much of anything. A ghostly hole an inch and a half across seemed to char itself in the program. As if my eye were right up against it, I saw in vivid memory what I'd seen the two times I'd dared a peek through the hole in the curtain: a bevy of ladies in masks and Nell Gwyn dresses and men in King Charles knee-breeches and long curled hair, and the second time a bunch of people and creatures just wild: all sorts and colors of clothes, humans with hoofs for feet and antennae springing from their foreheads, furry and feathery things that had more arms than two and in one case that many heads—as if they were dressed up in our Tempest,

Peer Gynt and Insect People costumes and some more besides.

Naturally I'd had mind-wavery fits both times. Afterwards Sid had wagged a finger at me and explained that on those two nights we'd been giving performances for people who'd arranged a costume theater-party and been going to attend a masquerade ball, and 'zounds, when would I learn to guard my half-patched pate?

I don't know, I guess never, I answered now, quick looking at a Giants pennant, a Korvette ad, a map of Central Park, my Willy Mays baseball and a Radio City tour ticket. That was eight items I'd looked at this trip without feeling any inward improvement. They weren't reassuring me at all.

The blue fly came slowly buzzing down over my screen and I asked it, "What are you looking for? A spider?" when what should I hear coming back through the dressing room straight toward my sleeping closet but Miss Nefer's footsteps. No one else walks that way.

She's going to do something to you, Greta, I thought. She's the maniac in the company. She's the one who terrorized you with the boning knife in the shrubbery, or sicked the giant tarantula on you at the dark end of the subway platform, or whatever it was, and the others are covering up for. She's going to smile the devil-smile and weave those white twig-fingers at you, all eight of them. And

Birnam Wood'll come to Dunsinane and you'll be burnt at the stake by men in armor or drawn and quartered by eight-legged monkeys that talk or torn apart by wild centaurs or whirled through the roof to the moon without being dressed for it or sent burrowing into the past to stifle in Iowa 1948 or Egypt 4,008 B.C. The screen won't keep her out.

Then a head of hair pushed over the screen. But it was black-bound-with-silver, Brahma bless us, and a moment later Martin was giving me one of his rare smiles.

I said, "Marty, do something for me. Don't ever use Miss Nefer's footsteps again. Her voice, okay, if you have to. But not the footsteps. Don't ask me why, just don't."

Martin came around and sat on the foot of my cot. My legs were already doubled up. He straightened out his blue-and-gold skirt and rested a hand on my black sneakers.

troop

"Feeling a little wonky, Greta?" he asked. "Don't worry about me. Banquo's dead and so's his ghost. We've finished the Banquet Scene. I've got lots of time."

I just looked at him, queerly I guess. Then without lifting my head I asked him, "Martin, tell me the truth. Does the dressing room move around?"

I was talking so low that he hitched a little closer, not touching me anywhere else though.

"The Earth's whipping around the sun at 20 miles a second," he replied, "and the dressing room goes with it."

I shook my head, my cheek scrubbing the pillow, "I mean ... shifting," I said. "By itself."

"How?" he asked.

"Well," I told him, "I've had this idea—it's just a sort of fancy, remember—that if you wanted to time-travel and, well, do things, you could hardly pick a more practical machine than a dressing room and sort of stage and half-theater attached, with actors to man it. Actors can fit in anywhere. They're used to learning new parts and wearing strange costumes. Heck, they're even used to traveling a lot. And if an actor's a bit strange nobody thinks anything of it—he's almost expected to be foreign, it's an asset to him."

"And a theater, well, a theater can spring up almost anywhere and nobody ask questions, except the zoning authorities and such and they can always be squared. Theaters come and go. It happens all the time. They're transitory. Yet theaters are crossroads, anonymous meeting places, anybody with a few bucks or sometimes nothing at all can go. And theaters attract important people, the sort of people you might want to do something to. Caesar was stabbed in a theater. Lincoln was shot in one. And...."

My voice trailed off. "A cute idea," he commented.

I reached down to his hand on my shoe and took hold of his middle finger as a baby might.

"Yeah," I said, "But Martin, is it true?"

He asked me gravely, "What do you think?"

I didn't say anything.

"How would you like to work in a company like that?" he asked speculatively.

"I don't really know," I said.

He sat up straighter and his voice got brisk. "Well, all fantasy aside, how'd you like to work in this company?" He asked, lightly slapping my ankle. "On the stage, I mean. Sid thinks you're ready for some of the smaller parts. In fact, he asked me to put it to you. He thinks you never take him seriously."

"Pardon me while I gasp and glow," I said. Then, "Oh Marty, I can't really imagine myself doing the tiniest part."

"Me neither, eight months ago," he said. "Now, look. Lady Macbeth."

"But Marty," I said, reaching for his finger again, "you haven't answered my question. About whether it's true."

"Oh that!" he said with a laugh, switching his hand to the other side. "Ask me something else."

"Okay," I said, "why am I bugged on the number eight? Because I'm permanently behind a private 8-ball?"

"Eight's a number with many properties," he said, suddenly as intently serious as he usually is. "The corners of a cube."

"You mean I'm a square?" I said. "Or just a brick? You know, 'She's a brick.'"

"But eight's most curious property," he continued with a frown, "is that lying on its side it signifies infinity. So eight erect is really—" and suddenly his made-up, naturally solemn face got a great glow of inspiration and devotion—"Infinity Arisen!"

Well, I don't know. You meet quite a few people in the theater who are bats on numerology, they use it to pick stage-names. But I'd never have guessed it of Martin. He always struck me as the skeptical, cynical type.

"I had another idea about eight," I said hesitatingly. "Spiders. That 8-legged asterisk on Miss Nefer's forehead—" I suppressed a shudder.

"You don't like her, do you?" he stated.

"I'm afraid of her," I said.

"You shouldn't be. She's a very great woman and tonight she's playing an infinitely more difficult part than I am. No, Greta," he went on as I started to protest, "believe me, you don't understand anything about it at this moment. Just as you don't understand about spiders, fearing them. They're the first to climb the rigging and to climb ashore too.

They're the web-weavers, the line-throwers, the connectors, Siva and Kali united in love. They're the double mandala, the beginning and the end, infinity mustered and on the march—"

"They're also on my New York screen!" I squeaked, shrinking back across the cot a little and pointing at a tiny glinting silver-and-black thing mounting below my Willy-ball.

Martin gently caught its line on his finger and lifted it very close to his face. "Eight eyes too," he told me. Then, "Poor little god," he said and put it back.

"Marty? Marty?" Sid's desperate stage-whisper rasped the length of the dressing room.

Martin stood up. "Yes, Sid?"

Sid's voice stayed a whisper but went from desperate to ferocious. "You villainous elf-skin! Know you not the Cauldron Scene's been playing a hundred heartbeats? 'Tis 'most my entrance and we still mustering only two witches out of three! Oh, you nott-pated starveling!"

Before Sid had got much more than half of that out, Martin had slipped around the screen, raced the length of the dressing room, and I'd heard a lusty thwack as he went out the door. I couldn't help grinning, though with Martin racked by anxieties and reliefs over his first time as Lady Mack, it was easy to understand it slipping his mind that he was still doubling Second Witch.

VI

I will vault credit
and affect high pleasures
Beyond death. —Ferdinand

I sat down where Martin had been, first pushing the screen far enough to the side for me to see the length of the dressing room and notice anyone coming through the door and any blurs moving behind the thin white curtain shutting off the boys' two-thirds.

I'd been going to think. But instead I just sat there, experiencing my body and the room around it, steadying myself or maybe readying myself. I couldn't tell which, but it was nothing to think about, only to feel. My heartbeat became a very faint, slow, solid throb. My spine straightened.

No one came in or went out. Distantly I heard Macbeth and the witches and the apparitions talk.

Once I looked at the New York Screen, but all the stuff there had grown stale. No protection, no nothing.

I reached down to my suitcase and from where I'd been going to get a miltown I took a dexedrine and popped it in my mouth. Then I started out, beginning to shake.

When I got to the end of the curtain I went around it to Sid's dressing table and asked Shakespeare, "Am I doing the right thing, Pop?"

But he didn't answer me out of his portrait. He just looked sneaky-innocent, like he knew a lot but wouldn't tell, and I found myself think of a little silver-framed photo Sid had used to keep there too of a cocky German-looking young actor with "Erich" autographed across it in white ink. At least I supposed he was an actor. He looked a little like Erich von Stroheim, but nicer yet somehow nastier too. The photo had used to upset me, I don't know why. Sid must have noticed it, for one day it was gone.

I thought of the tiny black-and-silver spider crawling across the remembered silver frame, and for some reason it gave me the cold creeps.

Well, this wasn't doing me any good, just making me feel dismal again, so I quickly went out. In the door I had to slip around the actors coming back from the Cauldron Scene and the big bolt nicked my hip.

Outside Maud was peeling off her Third Witch stuff to reveal Lady Macduff beneath. She twitched me a grin.

"How's it going?" I asked.

"Okay, I guess," she shrugged. "What an audience! Noisy as highschool kids."

"How come Sid didn't have a boy do your part?" I asked.

"He goofed, I guess. But I've battened down my bosoms and playing Mrs. Macduff as a boy."

"How does a girl do that in a dress?" I asked.

"She sits stiff and thinks pants," she said, handing me her witch robe. "'Scuse me now. I got to find my children and go get murdered."

I'd moved a few steps nearer the stage when I felt the gentlest tug at my hip. I looked down and saw that a taut black thread from the bottom of my sweater connected me with the dressing room. It must have snagged on the big bolt and unraveled. I moved my body an inch or so, tugging it delicately to see what it felt like and I got the answers: Theseus's clew, a spider's line, an umbilicus.

I reached down close to my side and snapped it with my fingernails. The black thread leaped away. But the dressing room door didn't vanish, or the wings change, or the world end, and I didn't fall down.

After that I just stood there for quite a while, feeling my new freedom and steadiness, letting my body get used to it. I didn't do any thinking. I hardly bothered to study anything around me, though I did notice that there were more bushes and trees than set pieces, and that the flickery lightning was simply torches and that Queen Elizabeth was in (or back in) the audience. Sometimes letting your body get used to something is all you should do, or maybe can do.

And I did smell horse dung.

When the Lady Macduff Scene was over and the Chicken Scene well begun, I went back to the dressing room. Actors call it the Chicken Scene because Macduff weeps in it about "all my pretty chickens and their dam," meaning his kids and wife, being murdered "at one fell swoop" on orders of that chickenyard-raiding "hell-kite" Macbeth.

Inside the dressing room I steered down the boys' side. Doc was putting on an improbable-looking dark makeup for Macbeth's last faithful servant Seyton. He didn't seem as boozy-woozy as usual for Fourth Act, but just the same I stopped to help him get into a chain-mail shirt made of thick cord woven and silvered.

In the third chair beyond, Sid was sitting back with his corset loosened and critically surveying Martin, who'd now changed to a white wool nightgown that clung and draped beautifully, but not particularly enticingly, on him and his folded towel, which had slipped a bit.

From beside Sid's mirror, Shakespeare smiled out of his portrait at them like an intelligent big-headed bug.

Martin stood tall, spread his arms rather like a high priest, and intoned, "Amici! Romani! Populares!"

I nudged Doc. "What goes on now?" I whispered.

He turned a bleary eye on them. "I think they are rehearsing Julius Caesar in Latin." He shrugged. "It begins the oration of Antony."

"But why?" I asked. Sid does like to put every moment to use when the performance-fire is in people, but this project seemed pretty far afield—hyper-pedantic. Yet at the same time I felt my scalp shivering as if my mind were jumping with speculations just below the surface.

Doc shook his head and shrugged again.

Sid shoved a palm at Martin and roared softly, "'Sdeath, boy, thou'rt not playing a Roman statua but a Roman! Loosen your knees and try again."

Then he saw me. Signing Martin to stop, he called, "Come hither, sweetling." I obeyed quickly. He gave me a fiendish grin and said, "Thou'st heard our proposal from Martin. What sayest thou, wench?"

This time the shiver was in my back. It felt good. I realized I was grinning back at him, and I knew what I'd been getting ready for the last twenty minutes.

"I'm on," I said. "Count me in the company."

Sid jumped up and grabbed me by the shoulders and hair and bussed me on both cheeks. It was a little like being bombed.

"Prodigious!" he cried. "Thou'lt play the Gentlewoman in the Sleepwalking Scene tonight. Martin, her costume! Now sweet wench, mark me well." His voice grew grave and old. "When was it she last walked?"

The new courage went out of me like water down a chute. "But Siddy, I can't start tonight," I protested, half pleading, half outraged.

"Tonight or never! 'Tis an emergency—we're short-handed." Again his voice changed. "When was it she last walked?"

"But Siddy, I don't know the part."

"You must. You've heard the play twenty times this year past. When was it she last walked?"

Martin was back and yanking down a blonde wig on my head and shoving my arms into a light gray robe.

"I've never studied the lines," I squeaked at Sidney.

"Liar! I've watched your lips move a dozen nights when you watched the scene from the wings. Close your eyes, girl! Martin, unhand her. Close your eyes, girl, empty your mind, and listen, listen only. When was it she last walked?"

In the blackness I heard myself replying to that cue, first in a whisper, then more loudly, then full-throated but grave, "Since his majesty went into the field, I have seen her rise from her bed, throw her nightgown upon her, unlock her closet, take forth—"

"Bravissimo!" Siddy cried and bombed me again. Martin hugged his arm around my shoulders too, then quickly stooped to start hooking up my robe from the bottom.

"But that's only the first lines, Siddy," I protested.

"They're enough!"

"But Siddy, what if I blow up?" I asked.

"Keep your mind empty. You won't. Further, I'll be at your side, doubling the Doctor, to prompt you if you pause."

That ought to take care of two of me, I thought. Then something else struck me. "But Siddy," I quavered, "how do I play the Gentlewoman as a boy?"

"Boy?" he demanded wonderingly. "Play her without falling down flat on your face and I'll be past measure happy!" And he smacked me hard on the fanny.

Martin's fingers were darting at the next to the last hook. I stopped him and shoved my hand down the neck of my sweater and got hold of the subway token and the chain it was on and yanked. It burned my neck but the gold links parted. I started to throw it across the room, but instead I smiled at Siddy and dropped it in his palm.

"The Sleepwalking Scene!" Maud hissed insistently to us from the door.

VII

I know death hath ten thousand several doors
For men to take their exits, and 'tis found

They go on such strange geometrical hinges,
You may open them both ways.—The Duchess

There is this about an actor on stage: he can see
the audience but he can't look at them, unless he's
a narrator or some sort of comic. I wasn't the first
(Grendel groks!) and only scared to death of
becoming the second as Siddy walked me out of the
wings onto the stage, over the groundcloth that felt
so much like ground, with a sort of interweaving
policeman-grip on my left arm.

Sid was in a dark gray robe looking like some
dismal kind of monk, his head so hooded for the
Doctor that you couldn't see his face at all.

My skull was pulse-buzzing. My throat was
squeezed dry. My heart was pounding. Below that
my body was empty, squirmy, electricity-stung, yet
with the feeling of wearing ice cold iron pants.

I heard as if from two million miles, "When was
it she last walked?" and then an iron bell
somewhere tolling the reply—I guess it had to be
my voice coming up through my body from my iron
pants: "Since his majesty went into the field—" and
so on, until Martin had come on stage, stary-eyed,
a white scarf tossed over the back of his long black
wig and a flaring candle two inches thick gripped in
his right hand and dripping wax on his wrist, and
started to do Lady Mack's sleepwalking half-hinted
confessions of the murders of Duncan and Banquo
and Lady Macduff.

So here is what I saw then without looking, like a vivid scene that floats out in front of your mind in a reverie, hovering against a background of dark blur, and sort of flashes on and off as you think, or in my case act. All the time, remember, with Sid's hand hard on my wrist and me now and then tolling Shakespearan language out of some lightless storehouse of memory I'd never known was there to belong to me.

There was a medium-size glade in a forest. Through the half-naked black branches shone a dark cold sky, like ashes of silver, early evening.

The glade had two horns, as it were, narrowing back to either side and going off through the forest. A chilly breeze was blowing out of them, almost enough to put out the candle. Its flame rippled.

Rather far back in the horn to my left, but not very far, were clumped two dozen or so men in dark cloaks they huddled around themselves. They wore brimmed tallish hats and pale stuff showing at their necks. Somehow I assumed that these men must be the "rude fellows from the City" I remembered Beau mentioning a million or so years ago. Although I couldn't see them very well, and didn't spend much time on them, there was one of them who had his hat off or excitedly pushed way back, showing a big pale forehead. Although that was all the conscious impression I had of his face, he seemed frighteningly familiar.

In the horn to my right, which was wider, were lined up about a dozen horses, with grooms holding tight every two of them, but throwing their heads back now and then as they strained against the reins, and stamping their front hooves restlessly. Oh, they frightened me, I tell you, that line of two-foot-long glossy-haired faces, writhing back their upper lips from teeth wide as piano keys, every horse of them looking as wild-eyed and evil as Fuseli's steed sticking its head through the drapes in his picture "The Nightmare."

To the center the trees came close to the stage. Just in front of them was Queen Elizabeth sitting on the chair on the spread carpet, just as I'd seen her out there before; only now I could see that the braziers were glowing and redly high-lighting her pale cheeks and dark red hair and the silver in her dress and cloak. She was looking at Martin—Lady Mack—most intently, her mouth grimaced tight, twisting her fingers together.

Standing rather close around her were a half dozen men with fancier hats and ruffs and wide-flaring riding gauntlets.

Then, through the trees and tall leafless bushes just behind Elizabeth, I saw an identical Elizabeth-face floating, only this one was smiling a demonic smile. The eyes were open very wide. Now and then the pupils darted rapid glances from side to side.

There was a sharp pain in my left wrist and Sid whisper-snarling at me, "Accustomed action!" out of the corner of his shadowed mouth.

I tolled on obediently, "It is an accustomed action with her, to seem thus washing her hands: I have known her continue in this a quarter of an hour."

Martin had set down the candle, which still flared and guttered, on a little high table so firm its thin legs must have been stabbed into the ground. And he was rubbing his hands together slowly, continually, tormentedly, trying to get rid of Duncan's blood which Mrs. Mack knows in her sleep is still there. And all the while as he did it, the agitation of the seated Elizabeth grew, the eyes flicking from side to side, hands writhing.

He got to the lines, "Here's the smell of blood still: all the perfumes of Arabia will not sweeten this little hand. Oh, oh, oh!"

As he wrung out those soft, tortured sighs, Elizabeth stood up from her chair and took a step forward. The courtiers moved toward her quickly, but not touching her, and she said loudly, "Tis the blood of Mary Stuart whereof she speaks—the pails of blood that will gush from her chopped neck. Oh, I cannot endure it!" And as she said that last, she suddenly turned about and strode back toward the trees, kicking out her ash-colored skirt. One of the courtiers turned with her and stooped toward her closely, whispering something. But although she paused a moment, all she said was, "Nay, Eyes, stop not the play, but follow me not! Nay, I say leave me, Leicester!" And she walked into the trees, he looking after her.

Then Sid was kicking my ankle and I was reciting something and Martin was taking up his candle again without looking at it saying with a drugged agitation, "To bed; to bed; there's knocking at the gate."

Elizabeth came walking out of the trees again, her head bowed. She couldn't have been in them ten seconds. Leicester hurried toward her, hand anxiously outstretched.

Martin moved offstage, torturedly yet softly wailing, "What's done cannot be undone."

Just then Elizabeth flicked aside Leicester's hand with playful contempt and looked up and she was smiling the devil-smile. A horse whinnied like a trumpeted snicker.

As Sid and I started our last few lines together I intoned mechanically, letting words free-fall from my mind to my tongue. All this time I had been answering Lady Mack in my thoughts, That's what you think, sister.

VIII

God cannot effect that anything which is past should not have been.

It is more impossible than rising the dead.—Summa Theologica

The moment I was out of sight of the audience I broke away from Sid and ran to the dressing room. I flopped down on the first chair I saw, my head and arms trailed over its back, and I almost passed out. It wasn't a mind-wavery fit. Just normal faint.

I couldn't have been there long—well, not very long, though the battle-rattle and alarums of the last scene were echoing tinnily from the stage—when Bruce and Beau and Mark (who was playing Malcolm, Martin's usual main part) came in wearing their last-act stage-armor and carrying between them Queen Elizabeth flaccid as a sack. Martin came after them, stripping off his white wool nightgown so fast that buttons flew. I thought automatically, I'll have to sew those.

They laid her down on three chairs set side by side and hurried out. Unpinning the folded towel, which had fallen around his waist, Martin walked over and looked down at her. He yanked off his wig by a braid and tossed it at me.

I let it hit me and fall on the floor. I was looking at that white queenly face, eyes open and staring sightless at the ceiling, mouth open a little too with a thread of foam trailing from the corner, and at that ice-cream-cone bodice that never stirred. The blue fly came buzzing over my head and circled down toward her face.

"Martin," I said with difficulty, "I don't think I'm going to like what we're doing."

He turned on me, his short hair elfed, his fists planted high on his hips at the edge of his black tights, which now were all his clothes.

"You knew!" he said impatiently. "You knew you were signing up for more than acting when you said, 'Count me in the company.'"

Like a legged sapphire the blue fly walked across her upper lip and stopped by the thread of foam.

"But Martin ... changing the past ... dipping back and killing the real queen ... replacing her with a double—"

His dark brows shot up. "The real—You think this is the real Queen Elizabeth?" He grabbed a bottle of rubbing alcohol from the nearest table, gushed some on a towel stained with grease-paint and, holding the dead head by its red hair (no, wig—the real one wore a wig too) scrubbed the forehead.

The white cosmetic came away, showing sallow skin and on it a faint tattoo in the form of an "S" styled like a yin-yang symbol left a little open.

"Snake!" he hissed. "Destroyer! The arch-enemy, the eternal opponent! God knows how many times people like Queen Elizabeth have been dug out of the past, first by Snakes, then by Spiders, and kidnapped or killed and replaced in the course of our war. This is the first big operation I've been on, Greta. But I know that much."

My head began to ache. I asked, "If she's an enemy double, why didn't she know a performance of Macbeth in her lifetime was an anachronism?"

"Foxholed in the past, only trying to hold a position, they get dulled. They turn half zombie. Even the Snakes. Even our people. Besides, she almost did catch on, twice when she spoke to Leicester."

"Martin," I said dully, "if there've been all these replacements, first by them, then by us, what's happened to the real Elizabeth?"

He shrugged. "God knows."

I asked softly, "But does He, Martin? Can He?"

He hugged his shoulders in, as if to contain a shudder. "Look, Greta," he said, "it's the Snakes who are the warpers and destroyers. We're restoring the past. The Spiders are trying to keep things as first created. We only kill when we must."

I shuddered then, for bursting out of my memory came the glittering, knife-flashing, night-shrouded, bloody image of my lover, the Spider soldier-of-change Erich von Hohenwald, dying in the grip of a giant silver spider, or spider-shaped entity large as he, as they rolled in a tangled ball down a flight of rocks in Central Park.

But the memory-burst didn't blow up my mind, as it had done a year ago, no more than snapping the black thread from my sweater had ended the world. I asked Martin, "Is that what the Snakes say?"

"Of course not! They make the same claims we do. But somewhere, Greta, you have to trust." He put out the middle finger of his hand.

I didn't take hold of it. He whirled it away, snapping it against his thumb.

"You're still grieving for that carrion there!" he accused me. He jerked down a section of white curtain and whirled it over the stiffening body. "If you must grieve, grieve for Miss Nefer! Exiled, imprisoned, locked forever in the past, her mind pulsing faintly in the black hole of the dead and gone, yearning for Nirvana yet nursing one lone painful patch of consciousness. And only to hold a fort! Only to make sure Mary Stuart is executed, the Armada licked, and that all the other consequences flow on. The Snakes' Elizabeth let Mary live ... and England die ... and the Spaniard hold North America to the Great Lakes and New Scandinavia."

Once more he put out his middle finger.

"All right, all right," I said, barely touching it. "You've convinced me."

"Great!" he said. "'By for now, Greta. I got to help strike the set."

"That's good," I said. He loped out.

I could hear the skirling sword-clashes of the final fight to the death of the two Macks, Duff and Beth. But I only sat there in the empty dressing room pretending to grieve for a devil-smiling snow tiger locked in a time-cage and for a cute sardonic German killed for insubordination that I had reported ... but really grieving for a girl who for a year had been a rootless child of the theater with a whole company of mothers and fathers, afraid of nothing more than subway bogies and Park and Village monsters.

As I sat there pitying myself beside a shrouded queen, a shadow fell across my knees. I saw stealing through the dressing room a young man in worn dark clothes. He couldn't have been more than twenty-three. He was a frail sort of guy with a weak chin and big forehead and eyes that saw everything. I knew at one he was the one who had seemed familiar to me in the knot of City fellows.

He looked at me and I looked from him to the picture sitting on the reserve makeup box by Siddy's mirror. And I began to tremble.

He looked at it too, of course, as fast as I did. And then he began to tremble too, though it was a finer-grained tremor than mine.

The sword-fight had ended seconds back and now I heard the witches faintly wailing, "Fair is foul, and foul is fair—" Sid has them echo that line offstage at the end to give a feeling of prophecy fulfilled.

Then Sid came pounding up. He's the first finished, since the fight ends offstage so Macduff can carry back a red-necked papier-mache head of him and show it to the audience. Sid stopped dead in the door.

Then the stranger turned around. His shoulders jerked as he saw Sid. He moved toward him just two or three steps at a time, speaking at the same time in breathy little rushes.

Sid stood there and watched him. When the other actors came boiling up behind him, he put his hands on the doorframe to either side so none of them could get past. Their faces peered around him.

And all this while the stranger was saying, "What may this mean? Can such things be? Are all the seeds of time ... wetted by some hell-trickle ... sprouted at once in their granary? Speak ... speak! You played me a play ... that I am writing in my secretest heart. Have you disjointed the frame of things ... to steal my unborn thoughts? Fair is foul indeed. Is all the world a stage? Speak, I say! Are you not my friend Sidney James Lessingham of King's Lynn ... singed by time's fiery wand ... sifted over with the ashes of thirty years? Speak, are you not he? Oh, there are more things in heaven and earth ... aye, and perchance hell too ... Speak, I charge you!"

And with that he put his hands on Sid's shoulders, half to shake him, I think, but half to keep from falling over. And for the one time I ever saw it, glib old Siddy had nothing to say.

He worked his lips. He opened his mouth twice and twice shut it. Then, with a kind of desperation in his face, he motioned the actors out of the way behind him with one big arm and swung the other around the stranger's narrow shoulders and swept him out of the dressing room, himself following.

The actors came pouring in then, Bruce tossing Macbeth's head to Martin like a football while he tugged off his horned helmet, Mark dumping a stack of shields in the corner, Maudie pausing as she skittered past me to say, "Hi Gret, great you're back," and patting my temple to show what part of me she meant. Beau went straight to Sid's dressing table and set the portrait aside and lifted out Sid's reserve makeup box.

"The lights, Martin!" he called.

Then Sid came back in, slamming and bolting the door behind him and standing for a moment with his back against it, panting.

I rushed to him. Something was boiling up inside me, but before it could get to my brain I opened my mouth and it came out as, "Siddy, you can't fool me, that was no dirty S-or-S. I don't care how much he shakes and purrs, or shakes a spear, or just plain shakes—Siddy, that was Shakespeare!"

"Aye, girl, I think so," he told me, holding my wrists together. "They can't find dolls to double men like that—or such is my main hope." A big sickly grin came on his face. "Oh, gods," he demanded, "with what words do you talk to a man whose speech you've stolen all your life?"

I asked him, "Sid, were we ever in Central Park?"

He answered, "Once—twelve months back. A one-night stand. They came for Erich. You flipped."

He swung me aside and moved behind Beau. All the lights went out.

Then I saw, dimly at first, the great dull-gleaming jewel, covered with dials and green-glowing windows, that Beau had lifted from Sid's reserve makeup box. The strongest green glow showed his intent face, still framed by the long glistening locks of the Ross wig, as he knelt before the thing—Major Maintainer, I remembered it was called.

"When now? Where?" Beau tossed impatiently to Sid over his shoulder.

"The forty-fourth year before our Lord's birth!" Sid answered instantly. "Rome!"

Beau's fingers danced over the dials like a musician's, or a safe-cracker's. The green glow flared and faded flickeringly.

"There's a storm in that vector of the Void."

"Circle it," Sid ordered.

"There are dark mists every way."

"Then pick the likeliest dark path!"

I called through the dark, "Fair is foul, and foul is fair, eh, Siddy?"

"Aye, chick," he answered me. "'Tis all the rule we have!"